In Our Backyard Garden

POEMS BY
Eileen Spinelli

PICTURES BY
Marcy Ramsey

Simon & Schuster Books for Young Readers
New York   London   Toronto   Sydney   Singapore

To the aunts: Rose, Eleanor,
Connie, Rita, Betty, Audrey, Jussie,
Norma, and both Marys. And the
uncles: Butch, Russell, Sonny,
Jimmy, Tommy, Mike, Jack, Tom,
and Pat. And to all the cousins . . .
especially Mark, Joni, and Geri.
—E. S.

To Maggi, best mother in the world!
—M. R.

SIMON & SCHUSTER BOOKS FOR YOUNG READERS
An imprint of Simon & Schuster Children's Publishing Division
1230 Avenue of the Americas, New York, New York 10020
Text copyright © 2004 by Eileen Spinelli
Illustrations copyright © 2004 by Marcy Ramsey
All rights reserved, including the right of reproduction in whole or in part in any form.
SIMON & SCHUSTER BOOKS FOR YOUNG READERS is a trademark of Simon & Schuster.
Book design by Greg Stadnyk
The text for this book is set in Italia.
The illustrations for this book are rendered in watercolor and oil pastel.
Manufactured in China
2 4 6 8 10 9 7 5 3 1
CIP data for this book is available from the Library of Congress.
ISBN 0-689-82666-4

first
edition

VERSES FROM OUR GARDEN

ON THE DAY MY BABY BROTHER IS BORN
WE PLANT A TREE IN HIS HONOR

•

HAIRCUT

•

BABY BROTHER'S FIRST LOOK AT THE NIGHT SKY

•

FAMILY PICNIC

•

GRANDDAD MAKES USE OF THE HANDKERCHIEF WAYNE
NEWTON TOSSED TO GRANDMOTHER IN 1998 AND
ALMOST ENDS UP IN DIVORCE COURT

•

AUNT SISSY WILL MARRY POSTMAN JOE IN THE SPRING—
HERE'S HOW THEY MET

•

PERFECT

•

JACK-O'-LANTERN

•

LEAVES

•

FIRST SNOW

•

ALMOST CHRISTMAS

•

GRANDDAD HAS A COLD

•

THE FIRST CROCUS

•

THE MORNING OF AUNT SISSY'S WEDDING

•

AUNT LOIS LEARNS TO DRIVE

•

PLANTING A TREE FOR GRANDDAD'S BIRTHDAY

•

BEDTIME

ON THE DAY MY BABY BROTHER IS BORN WE PLANT A TREE IN HIS HONOR

Oh, my baby brother,
even the garden spiders
spin you a welcome
on their sun-dotted webs
as Granddad and I
dig a hole for your tree.
Mom and Dad choose a white birch
because it was a poet's favorite.
He wrote a poem called "Birches."
Grandmother promises to read it aloud
one night—here in the backyard
under your tree. To both of us.
On the blue blanket.
By moonlight.

HAIRCUT

Since Dad lost his job,
Mom's been cutting his hair
to save money.
Dad carries a chair
from the kitchen,
sits in the middle of the yard.
Snip. Snip. Snip. Go the scissors.
"Don't nip my ear," says Dad.
Mom grins.
Hair flits,
flies,
falls onto the grass.
No sweeping up—
the birds will whisk
Dad's hair away,
weave it like soft
brown threads
into their nests.

BABY BROTHER'S FIRST LOOK AT THE NIGHT SKY

Before you even know
the word for sky
or moon
or star,
Grandmother lifts you
from sleep,
carries you
down the hall,
calls everyone
to follow,
and we go
out the back door
into the honeysuckle dark.
Cicadas hum with heat.
Our feet are bare.
Aunt Sissy's nightgown
swims against the breeze.
Orion's belt is clear,
and there's the twinkling bear—
the little one.
Grandmother has made
stargazers
of us all.

FAMILY PICNIC

1.
The city relatives arrive.
Aunt Lois brings a bakery cake.
Uncle Henry brings pickles from the deli.
Cousin Liz brings another new boyfriend.
This one is Brian.
This one has an earring in his nose.

2.
Aunt Sissy and Aunt Lois aren't speaking much.
They had a falling out.
That's what Grandmother calls an argument.
They fell out in May.
They fell out over a beet,
a beet that dropped from Aunt Sissy's fork—
plop—onto Aunt Lois's lap.
A beet that ruined Aunt Lois's new white dress.

3.
Dad starts the grill.
Granddad shucks the corn.
Grandmother and I set the picnic table.
I put smooth rocks on the napkins,
so they won't blow away.
Mom brings food from the kitchen:
potato salad, deviled eggs, dilly green beans.
No beets.

4.
My baby brother cries.
He had been napping.
Mom brings him out to the picnic.
"Let me hold the little guy," says Uncle Henry.
Round the table they go—
Uncle Henry and my baby brother.
Bouncy! Bouncy! Bouncy!
BURP!
Baby brother spits up on
Brian's head.
I hold my breath.
What will Brian do?
Brian laughs.
Later I whisper to Cousin Liz,
"I like your Brian."

5.
The sun goes down.
Dad lights the outdoor lanterns.
Grandmother reads from "Birches."
"So was I once a swinger of birches.
And so I dream of going back to be . . ."
Granddad and Uncle Henry play checkers.
Aunt Lois kicks off her shoes,
teaches my mom a new dance step
on the cool, night-dark grass.
Aunt Sissy paints my toenails—
bright red.
Behind the garden shed
Cousin Liz and Brian are kissing.
I can see them—
all romantical.
Just like on TV.

GRANDDAD MAKES USE OF THE HANDKERCHIEF WAYNE NEWTON TOSSED TO GRANDMOTHER IN 1998 AND ALMOST ENDS UP IN DIVORCE COURT

Granddad
swears
he honestly
didn't know
the dazzling history
of the red handkerchief
when he cut it
into strips
with the garden shears
to hold up
his tomato plants.

AUNT SISSY WILL MARRY POSTMAN JOE IN THE SPRING— HERE'S HOW THEY MET

Aunt Sissy,
in pink curlers
and an old bathing suit,
was out back
picking peppers
when she saw a snake.
She screamed so loud
Postman Joe heard
from two blocks away.
Sudden hero,
he came running,
tripping over a bag of
fertilizer
right into Aunt Sissy's
waiting arms.

PERFECT

September's sun
falls golden
on the garden.
A butterfly
wings past
my baby brother.
Granddad picks
the last of
the zucchini.
Grandmother cuts
a last bouquet
of mint.
Aunt Sissy and I
take one last
hammock ride
to places we have
read about
in books.

And then Dad enters,
grinning,
through the gate:
He got a job today.
Mom twirls around
the birdbath
at the news.
Aunt Sissy's Joe
says: "Ice cream
all around"—
his treat.
I want to hug
the fading
golden light.
I do not want
this perfect day
to end.

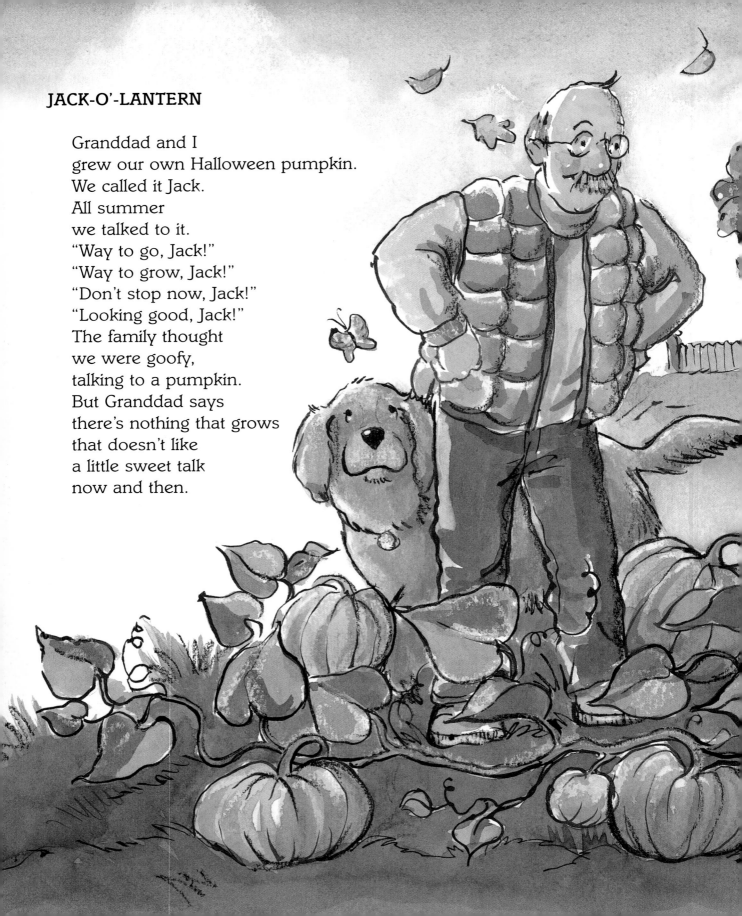

JACK-O'-LANTERN

Granddad and I
grew our own Halloween pumpkin.
We called it Jack.
All summer
we talked to it.
"Way to go, Jack!"
"Way to grow, Jack!"
"Don't stop now, Jack!"
"Looking good, Jack!"
The family thought
we were goofy,
talking to a pumpkin.
But Granddad says
there's nothing that grows
that doesn't like
a little sweet talk
now and then.

LEAVES

Fact: There are 200,000 leaves on one big tree.

Leaves.
Leaves.
And more leaves.
Everybody rakes.
Even the city relatives
have come to help.
It's hard work.
Granddad complains.
Grandmother gives him
one of her looks.
"Who planted all the trees?"
she says.
No more complaints
from Granddad.

FIRST SNOW

All night it snows.
And when we wake,
the yard is lovely
and adrift
in white.
Ragged rosebushes
near the shed
have blossomed
into flower puffs
of snow.
Aunt Sissy and I
slip bare feet
into boots.
Throw coats
over our pajamas.
Run into
the sweet
snowy air.

ALMOST CHRISTMAS

It's almost Christmas.
Granddad and I
cut pine branches,
holly boughs,
juniper bouquets.
We gather pinecones
into baskets,
then deliver
this wintry harvest
to the city relatives,
so they can decorate
their third-floor
apartment
with real stuff,
not plastic.

On the way home
we stop at a diner
for doughnuts
and hot chocolate.
Granddad leaves
the waitress a
sprig of holly
with the tip.

GRANDDAD HAS A COLD

Granddad hasn't been feeling well.
The doctor says for him to stay in bed.
Aunt Sissy's Joe brings Granddad a TV.
Granddad doesn't care for television.
Mom brings Granddad a book.
Granddad says reading hurts his eyes.
Aunt Sissy brings him a bowl of soup.
Granddad sighs, "Not hungry."

I think I know what Granddad wants.
He wants to see his garden.
We push his bed to the window.
Granddad brightens.
He waves to a winter cardinal.
He scolds a squirrel at the bird feeder.
He starts making plans for spring.

THE FIRST CROCUS

Mom and I
play a little game:
Whoever spies
the first crocus
gets treated to
an ice-cream cone.
That's how we
celebrate
the coming of spring.
Each morning
for weeks
I've rushed to
my window,
before I even
brush my teeth
or dress
or comb my hair.
One day it's there!
Almost hidden,
peeking from
beneath a bush—
first crocus,
purple as
an Easter basket bow.
I go to Mom's bedroom,
shake her awake.
"I win! I win!"
She grins a sleepy
smile:
"Chocolate or vanilla?"

THE MORNING OF AUNT SISSY'S WEDDING

Aunt Sissy is getting married today
in our backyard.
From neighbors we have borrowed
lawn chairs and folding tables.
Tulips and daffodils line
the path where Aunt Sissy will walk.
My dress is a cloud of pink
hanging on the closet door.
Dad bought bagels for breakfast.
No one is eating except Uncle Henry.
He's had four.
Mom notices the arbor needs a paint job,
but it's too late now.
Aunt Lois runs in and out—
screen door slapping—
so much to do before the minister comes.
Grandmother irons Aunt Sissy's satin slip.
Cousin Liz is doing Aunt Sissy's makeup.
Baby brother is howling for attention.
Brian's gone to pick up more ice.
Somebody turns on the radio:
possible showers this afternoon.
It had been Granddad's idea
to have Aunt Sissy's wedding
in the backyard.
And so he waves the weather-words away.
He tweaks my cheek. "Think sun," he says.
"Think sun."
And sun it is the whole sweet day.
The whole sweet day.

AUNT LOIS LEARNS TO DRIVE

Aunt Lois has decided
to learn to drive.
She wants Dad to teach her.
"Henry has no patience,"
she says.
First lesson:
Back out of the garage.
Not part of the lesson:
Scrape the fence.
Bump the azalea.
Squash four tulips.
Knock down the arbor.
Everyone runs,
shrieks.
Lesson over.
Later, Mom pats
Aunt Lois's arm.
"That arbor needed
a paint job anyway."

PLANTING A TREE FOR GRANDDAD'S BIRTHDAY

It's my idea—
to plant a tree for Granddad.
Hasn't he planted a tree
for each of us?
My own cherry tree
rustles a pink scented
Yes
and everyone agrees.
"A red maple," says Grandmother.
"He likes red maples."
So Dad and Uncle Henry drive
the old truck to the nursery.
Joe and Brian dig the hole.
I help.

Granddad takes the hose from Mom.
"Nobody waters like me," he says.
When the tree is finally planted,
we all hold hands around it
like in a circle game.
Aunt Sissy and Aunt Lois
hold each other's hand
and smile.
They have long since
fallen back in.
Brian holds my baby brother
in his arms.
Mom starts singing "Happy Birthday."
The rest of us join in.
Granddad wipes a tear away,
then laughs. "Today I feel
almost as young as this tree."

BEDTIME

Night raindrops
splash
sweet lullaby sounds.
Spring moonlight
puddles
the soft grass.
I stand under Granddad's
blue umbrella.
I wear my old rain boots.
Here, in my backyard garden
memories twinkle like stars.
I can easily
fill my pockets with them.
Soon, it will be bedtime.
But not for baby owl,
learning to fly
from our tallest tree,
trusting that
its feathered wings
are ready.